A WANDER IN THE WOODS

2021

Hidden Adventures

Edited By Iain McQueen

First published in Great Britain in 2021 by:

Young Writers
Remus House
Coltsfoot Drive
Peterborough
PE2 9BF
Telephone: 01733 890066
Website: www.youngwriters.co.uk

All Rights Reserved
Book Design by Ashley Janson
© Copyright Contributors 2021
Softback ISBN 978-1-80015-651-7

Printed and bound in the UK by BookPrintingUK
Website: www.bookprintinguk.com
YB0487F

FOREWORD

Welcome, Reader!

Are you ready to take a Wander in the Woods? Then come right this way - your journey to amazing adventures awaits. It's very simple, all you have to do is turn the page and you'll be transported into a forest brimming with super stories.

Is it magic? Is it a trick? No! It's all down to the skill and imagination of primary school pupils from around the country. We gave them the task of writing a story and to do it in just 100 words! I think you'll agree they've achieved that brilliantly – this book is jam-packed with exciting and thrilling tales, and such variety too, from mystical portals to creepy monsters lurking in the dark!

These young authors have brought their ideas to life using only their words. This is the power of creativity and it gives us life too! Here at Young Writers we want to pass our love of the written word onto the next generation and what better way to do that than to celebrate their writing by publishing it in a book!

It sets their work free from homework books and notepads and puts it where it deserves to be – out in the world and preserved forever! Each awesome author in this book should be super proud of themselves, and now they've got proof of their ideas and their creativity in black and white, to look back on in years to come!

CONTENTS

Al Mizan School, London

Umar Farooq (11)	1
Faris Abdirashid	2

Audley Junior School, Blackburn

Emaan Hussain (11)	3
Faliha Patel (11)	4
Eliina Khan (11)	5

Baildon CE Primary School, Baildon

Lucy Ellis-Heath (10)	6

Borden CE Primary School, Borden

Chloe Ward (7)	7
Emma Ebulue (8)	8
Daisy Thornby (7)	9
Henry Batchelor (8)	10
Kenneth Igbinedion (8)	11
Olivia Sutton (8)	12
Ada Lewis (8)	13
Dara Agunbiade (8)	14
Reuben Brown (7)	15
Liam Moore (7)	16
Connor Monk (7)	17
Freddy Bolton (8)	18
Thea Billington (8)	19
Jessica Barnden (8)	20
Connie Hambrook (7)	21
Isabelle Brown (8)	22
David Sofolabo (8)	23
Dolcie-Mae Arnold (8)	24
Nathaniel Igbaifua (8)	25
Ella Ebulue (8)	26

Cravenwood Primary Academy, Crumpsall

Zikra Lal (8)	27
Khadija Irfan (7)	28

Eccleston St Mary's CE Primary School, Eccleston

Piper Kirkwood-Wilson (8)	29
Daniel Traynor (8)	30
Leo Berto (8)	31
Theo Wright (8)	32
Grace Aspinall (8)	33
Jacob Redgrave (8)	34

ESMS Junior School, Edinburgh

Oscar Atkinson (8)	35
Matthew Goodbrand (9)	36
Giselle Lee (9)	37
Amber Cattanach (8)	38
Laila Dewar (8)	39
Erin O'Brien (9)	40
Junming Che (8)	41
Sophie Seddon (9)	42
Roddy Browne (9)	43
Lily Paulo (8)	44
Johnny Forbes (9)	45
Lucy Gammeli (9)	46

Friars Academy, Wellingborough

Ross Bailey (11)	47
Katie Jones (12)	48
Ben Lawrence (12)	49
Sienna Edwards (12)	50
Alex Adair (12)	51
Cordell Thomas (12)	52
Bradley Smith (11)	53
Stanley Martyne (12)	54

Grove Primary School, Wolverhampton

Grace Kwarteng (10)	55
Simran Kaur Gill (11)	56
Almaza	57
Louie Fellows (9)	58

Headlands Primary School, Northampton

Archie Brooksbank (11)	59
Kassie Teeboon (11)	60
Lola Claringbold (11)	61
Jovanna Jojo (11)	62
Greta Meskauskaite (11)	63
Aoife Collins (11)	64
Amy Heath (11)	65
Sara Sultan (11)	66
Lily Owen (11)	67
Irina Bilali (10)	68
Imran Ahmed (11)	69
Brackyn Joseph (11)	70
Max Knight (11)	71
Austin Seby (11)	72
Faith Preston-Nel (11)	73
Ruby Skelton (11)	74
Emily Owen (11)	75
Kaysah Rahman (11)	76
Evie Wilson (10)	77
Jay Evans	78
Evie Hamilton-Atkins (10)	79
Leo Hammond-Wood (10)	80
Kian Mcgee (10)	81
Skye England (11)	82
Keelan Crouch (11)	83
Yohan Aneesh (10)	84
Scarlett Handley (11)	85
Elwin Joy (11)	86
Ruby Stewart (11)	87
Omid Rasuli (10)	88
Kelsey Windram (11)	89
Mia Carter (10)	90

Holy Family Catholic Primary School, Ingol

Alessia de Molfetta-Page (10)	91
Myla Spencer (10)	92
Lena Siatka (10)	93
Klara Barbara Buczkowska (10)	94
Olivia Fryzowska (9)	95
Jack Fletcher (10)	96
Olivia Rudzka (10)	97

King Solomon International Business School, Birmingham

Varswati Das (10)	98

Lakeside Primary Academy, Frimley

Ulde Burleviciute (10)	99
Jayden Duffin (10)	100
Noah Brown (10)	101
Jake Seward (10)	102

Lenham Primary School, Lenham

Darcie Dunbar (9)	103

Ling Bob JI&N School, Pellon

Oliver Watson (10)	104
Megan Watson (11)	105

Merton Court Preparatory School, Sidcup

Tommaso Etemi (10)	106
Joachim Wong (10)	107
Onali Jayawardhena (10)	108
Priyanka Lall (10)	109
Olivya Isaac (10)	110
Aariya Patel (9)	111
Elinor Micklefield (10)	112
Lilia White (10)	113
Sofia Sarvestani (10)	114
Zara Enver (10)	115
Charlie Wilson (10)	116
Freddie Kite (10)	117
Daisy Cormack (10)	118
Christiaan Datema (10)	119
Satara Dhesi (10)	120
Ethan Pearce (10)	121
Keeya Pindoria (10)	122

Miles Coverdale Primary School, Shepherd's Bush

Maryam Akhmedova (11)	123
Ali Ahmad (11)	124
Retaj Ismail (11)	125
Rayan Anwar (11)	126
Musub Mohamoud (11)	127
Violett Guba (11)	128
Zakaria Gherbi (11)	129
Farah Elfayoumy (11)	130
Nadir Zumrawy (11)	131
Mustafa Abbasi (11)	132
Fatima Ali (11)	133
Medina Makhloufi (11)	134

Minster CE Primary School, Minster

Daisy-lou Czuczman (10)	135
Ameli Shaw (10)	136
Toby Woodward (9)	137
Ella Hooper (11)	138

Shirley Community Primary School, Cambridge

Samuel Garfoot (11)	139
Hapi Bonetti-Phillips (11)	140

St Francis Catholic Primary School, Maldon

Poppy Janes (8)	141

St George's CE Primary School, Wrotham

Harry Malone (10)	142
Charlie Newbold (9)	143
James Abbott (9)	144
Blake Saunders (10)	145
Benjamin Forsyth (10)	146
Ryan Puttock (10)	147
James Richards (10)	148
Lucy Hodges (9)	149

St Patrick's Primary School, Hilltown

Jamie Rooney McGuigan (10)	150
Cara Cole (10)	151
Erin Rooney (10)	152
Jessie Maginn (10)	153
CJ Grant (10)	154
Beibhinn McPolin (10)	155
Tj McKay (10)	156

St Thomas A Becket Catholic Primary School, Eastbourne

Mathushi Manoharan (9)	157
Eunice Macaranas (10)	158
Henry Leek (9)	159
George Prince (9)	160

Talavera Junior School, Gun Hill

Sehjta Chauhan (8)   161

Unity Academy, Blackpool

Amelia Southern (9)	162
Mia Thornber (9)	163
Jack Fearon (8)	164
Kacey Coulter (9)	165
Athena Mann (9)	166
Jack William Jones (10)	167
Lewis Geoghegan (9)	168
Kila Murphy (9)	169
Harry Abraham (10)	170

Windhill Primary School, Mexborough

Mena Chaiyapantho (8)	171
Ava Law (8)	172
George Farthing (8)	173
Jashan Kaur (7)	174

Ysgol Gymraeg Caerffili, Caerphilly

Isabella Ashford (10)   175

Ysgol Gynradd Gymunedol Gymraeg Llantrisant, Miskin

Briallen Davies (9)   176

THE STORIES

Finding My Strength

There must be a way out, right? I mean it's so dark here, can barely see, despite the morning light. The room's sucked up all the air greedily, not leaving any to share. Concentrate on listening to the squeals of laughter outside. Blackout thoughts, how I'm missing out on the fun, my body has denied. Her sneakers squeaking, a ball bouncing before it's dunked. And here I lie, defunct. Stuck in slow-mo. Reaching out for someone to catch me. Before I hit what's below. The malignant growth within me, taking over completely. Must be a way out, right?

Umar Farooq (11)
Al Mizan School, London

The Undercover Plot

I arrive at the secret meeting place. Swiftly checking for any followers, I punch in the code and the door swings open. Tucked away in the woods, it is the perfect place to do as you wish and speak comfortably with your friends without the eyes of others. I let out a gasp as I see my companions unconscious in a large pool of blood. I hear footsteps behind me and faint. I wake up in an area full of wires, instruments and faces of adults. I'm in a hospital, I release a gasp as I remember my stalker's face.

Faris Abdirashid
Al Mizan School, London

Lurking In The Shadows

The sun was starting to set and the forest looked different, I was afraid of what could be hiding in the shadows. A cold breeze passed by, making me shiver. I heard an unfamiliar sound which made me very cautious. My heart was racing and my legs started to shake. The sky was dotted with glistening stars and the moon shone like a diamond. Leaves on the ground rustled. The forest was now pitch-black.
Snap!
What was that? Who was there? I'm not alone in this mysterious forest? Oh no! I wonder what was lurking in the dark shadows...

Emaan Hussain (11)
Audley Junior School, Blackburn

Hidden Youth

I had arrived at the secret meeting place. It was a small brick hut, painted emerald in order to camouflage against the various assortment of viridian-coloured leaves. I took a step then hesitated. This was too risky. Maybe I should just call the police and let them deal with this. No, I had come this far. I wasn't about to back out now. I had to do this. For Saarah. I took a deep breath and hauled my backpack over my shoulder with a firm grip. I could do this. Turning the rusty handle, I thrust open the door...

Faliha Patel (11)
Audley Junior School, Blackburn

Faith In Humanity

It was getting dark, that's when I actually realised. I tried to brush it off in the woods but I could feel it, that negative energy haunting me. I then realised it was her, this whole time it had been. She never seemed the sort to hurt such innocent people, especially if they were just like her, invisible. I realised I had to protect myself, from her. I didn't see it. I had lost my faith in humanity. All because of her. You should never trust anyone or yourself, why? Because she was me this whole time.

Eliina Khan (11)
Audley Junior School, Blackburn

An Escape, Or Not...

There must be a way out. I've been in here for almost a month now. I've been thinking about escaping the whole time. It's been a few hours since lunch so it should be dinner soon. This place is hell. I don't even know why they sent me here, they just came and took me away one day. My parents demanded an explanation, but they didn't get anywhere. Suddenly, the fire alarm went off, we had been taught a drill if this happened. So we all marched to the meeting point, and in a second, the building was gone...

Lucy Ellis-Heath (10)
Baildon CE Primary School, Baildon

The Secret Door

Once a girl called Naya and a boy called Adam found a secret door. "Go in," said Adam.
"Are you sure?" mumbled Naya. "There is a ghost," screamed Naya.
The ghost said, "I am nice if you want to go home, give me a gift."
Adam said, "I remember a chest around here, I'll find a present."
They did and then they were teleported home.
"Back home," said Naya. "That was fun," said Naya.
"Yes, it was," said Adam. "Should we go and play?"
"Yes!"
"Race you!"
They told Mum about the story upstairs.

Chloe Ward (7)
Borden CE Primary School, Borden

Lila And The Fox

Once, there was a girl called Lila, she wanted to capture a fox so she went to the forest and placed traps, she saw a sign saying: *Secret*.
I'll probably find a fox, thought Lila. So she went down the path, the trees fell.
"Was that a trap?" She continued until she saw something. "A fox!" Lila said and she used one of her traps and caught him!
"Let me go!" said the fox.
"Only if you guide me out of here."
"Okay, I'll help you," cried the fox.
Then suddenly, Lila woke up, it was a dream.

Emma Ebulue (8)
Borden CE Primary School, Borden

The Girl Who Had A Power!

Once upon a time, a girl called Lily was in a forest, she had powers, she could talk to animals. She heard a call that said, "Lily, come now." She saw a cottage and stepped inside. There she saw cauldron pots and other magical ingredients as well as witches and skeletons, she was frightened, she hid behind a shelf of books. The witch put ingredients in the cauldron. Lily heard her say, "Where is the girl I was going to steal powers from?" Lily was so frightened she ran out of the cottage through the woods, straight back home safely.

Daisy Thornby (7)
Borden CE Primary School, Borden

Dragon Hunters

Once upon a time, there was a dragon called Sapphire who lived in an enchanted forest. A knight who wanted to be a wizard bought a spellbook and went to the enchanted forest to practise spells. Sir Wizard looked at his book and bumped into the dragon. The dragon was cross and fired an ice-ball at Sir Wizard. The knight used a shield spell on the ice-ball. Before the dragon could fire another ice-ball, the knight levitated the dragon into the air. A portal opened, showing a demon monster in a new dimension. They must work together to defeat him.

Henry Batchelor (8)
Borden CE Primary School, Borden

Lost In The Woods

Eren and Marco were walking through the woods and they saw a man chopping wood from the trees. The boys whispered, "Hello." The man turned around and took out his sword and yelled. "Quake bomb!" The boys got separated at the ends of the wood. Eren cried, "Where are you, big bro?" Eren searched for Marco high and low but he couldn't find him. Eren saw Marco's favourite dino toy that he took on the trip. Eren thought, he must be close. Eren heard a voice, Eren closer and closer and it led to Marco.

Kenneth Igbinedion (8)
Borden CE Primary School, Borden

The Woodland Dragon

Once upon a time, there was a little girl called Lilly and she went for a walk in the woods. Lilly was walking then she heard a noise, it sounded like a crash. Lilly ran and ran until she saw a magic wizard training a dragon. Lilly had a dragon book in her bag. On chapter three it said, 'All dragons have a magic ability'. Lilly ran to the wizard and said, "Excuse me, do you know the dragon's ability?"

"I do," said the wizard.

Then the dragon made the snow fall. Lilly called her Snowy.

Olivia Sutton (8)
Borden CE Primary School, Borden

Forest Island

Ella and Ada arrived at the dock and hopped onto their boat. An hour later, there was a storm. Both of them were looking for somewhere safe. Then in the distance, Ella saw an abandoned forest island. *Crack.* They quickly sailed forwards, heading for the island, when they arrived they started to collect wood for a campfire and began to build a shelter. It began to get dark so they decided to rest for the night. The next day as Ella was looking for food, she spotted a secret door. They were curious and opened it...

Ada Lewis (8)
Borden CE Primary School, Borden

Spy Girls

Once upon a time, there were two best friends called Emma and Zoe. Emma lived in a cabin in enchanted woods. When they were nine they discovered that they were secret agents working for Starvain. When they were 13, they'd completed four missions. But their fifth mission was finding their dad in Australia, where there was a place near the ocean. Emma's mum said, "Your dad is not here because he's hiding from us!" So by the end of the year, they found their dad in Poland. So they had a big party.

Dara Agunbiade (8)
Borden CE Primary School, Borden

The Forbidden Forest

Once upon a time in a forbidden forest, there were two campers called Izzy and Jacob. They found a portal but it was unlit. So they went exploring and found a forbidden temple. In the temple was a chest and Izzy opened it. There was flint and steel inside, they returned to the portal and lit it. Then went through into the hidden woods. In the distance was the legendary gem and they approached it. They used the legendary gem to save the world and be the heroes. They were famous but it got taken by monsters!

Reuben Brown (7)
Borden CE Primary School, Borden

The Castle

Once upon a time, there was a boy called Tom. He went on a walk in the woods with his mum and dad but he wandered off. Tom found a castle. Tom was a curious boy and he went into the castle. A Cyclops and Dracula lived there. They offered Tom dinner! It was also his favourite! But when Tom was having dinner, he noticed the time and told the Cyclops and Dracula, he should go home and they said, "Yes." So Tom quickly ran home and jumped into bed and when he woke up he thought he'd dreamed it.

Liam Moore (7)
Borden CE Primary School, Borden

To A New World

Once upon a time, I was wandering in the woods but then I saw something. I looked at it carefully and it was a portal. I walked closer and it sucked me in. I looked, there was nothing. Then I looked around again and saw lots of mythical creatures. There were unicorns, dragons and yetis. Then something started to chase me. I ran as fast as I could to the portal to escape. After I was out I ran home to my family and told them what happened but they didn't believe me. It was all in my imagination.

Connor Monk (7)
Borden CE Primary School, Borden

A Wander In The Woods

Once upon a time, me and my dad were walking in a dark, spooky forest. While we were there, I heard a noise behind me. It was just a rabbit running. A little while later, I found a swing. I wanted to go on it but it looked like it was going to break so we carried on. We lost track of time and it was night. We were lost, suddenly we were at the swing again and the rabbit was on it. The swing moved by itself and the rabbit shouted, "Freddy, there's a werewolf behind you!" I fainted.

Freddy Bolton (8)
Borden CE Primary School, Borden

The Walk

Emily was cycling to the forest to walk her dog. She stopped. The gate opened. After walking through, the gate slammed shut. Her dog started to bark, he stopped barking after he ate watermelon. She reached into her bag, deeper and deeper. She found a key that she'd brought and tried it on the gate lock. The gate opened wide. As she walked through the gate, she saw the forest cleaner. He was the one who opened the gate, so he could clear up the rubbish and leaves that were on the floor.

Thea Billington (8)
Borden CE Primary School, Borden

Escape From The Scary Maze

Me and my friend Daisy were playing in the woods when it was dark and scary. Someone came up to us very fast and put a bag over our heads. The men put us in a maze and locked the gate. The bags came off, we saw the maze was made of sticks and leaves. We tried to find the exit but then we lost each other. Daisy got out by climbing over the wall. Daisy called, "Left, right!" So I could escape. Daisy unlocked the door from the outside so I could get out then we hugged each other.

Jessica Barnden (8)
Borden CE Primary School, Borden

Sleeping Dragon

Once upon a time, there were two children, Max and Anabella, and a pixie. Anabella and Max had a magic chair. One day they went flying to Pixie Land. They got into the chair and they flew it to the woods and decided to live there. Max was collecting strawberries when he saw a dragon. Luckily another pixie came. It said its name was Mooula. She knew what the dragon was and wanted to help. She called Clodo the T-rex and Clodo gave special leaves to Max to make the dragon go to sleep.

Connie Hambrook (7)
Borden CE Primary School, Borden

The Helpful Friend

I found a spooky house in the haunted woods. I was very, very scared. I thought there were ghosts inside, so I took a big breath then I went inside. I walked into the hallway and I saw a vampire. I told the vampire that I was lost and he helped me find my way home. I did not want to leave the vampire so I hugged my vampire friend one last time. He quickly ran home to the spooky house for dinner, with his friends and family. I never saw him ever again. I really miss him right now.

Isabelle Brown (8)
Borden CE Primary School, Borden

The Escape Door

In the distance, I saw the escape door! All I had to do was walk out of the door and I could escape. But, as I walked towards it, something unusual happened. Scary Larry and his minions jumped out of the trees and bushes. Before all of the rustling noises had gone, they all started attacking me. From now on I felt guilty. All my friends were gone. When I had the chance to save them. I couldn't. Now it was time to avenge them. I took my baseball bat and they ran. I escaped.

David Sofolabo (8)
Borden CE Primary School, Borden

The Harry Potter Footsteps

I heard the turn of a key unlocking, it woke me up, myself and Lanni were enjoying our Harry Potter sleepover. Right in front of us, we saw a secret door. So we walked through the secret door. We screamed because it was the Forbidden Forest in Harry Potter. We went too far into the forest and then ran into Voldemort so we got our wands and battled bravely to see our families after we won the battle. We then wandered through the woods again until we saw the secret door again.

Dolcie-Mae Arnold (8)
Borden CE Primary School, Borden

The Magic Tea Party

Once upon a time, it was winter. I went on a walk in the cold woods. I started to walk, I did not know where I was. There was a hole in front of me in the ground. Something grabbed my ankle. The hole was too dark to see what it was. I fell into the hole. What I saw amazed me. I saw a magnificent doorway. I opened it and it led to a rainbow tea party and the thing that grabbed my leg was a fluffy, white, wintry rabbit.

Nathaniel Igbaifua (8)
Borden CE Primary School, Borden

Amy And The Three Aliens

One day, Amy went for a walk in a nearby forest, when she was walking she soon became tired and had a sandwich, she packed in her bag. After she ate, she began walking again. Suddenly, Amy saw a bright green light, she went to go find the light. Then she saw a UFO, then three aliens jumped out the UFO and the three aliens attacked Amy, but Amy defeated the aliens and sprinted out the forest and never returned.

Ella Ebulue (8)
Borden CE Primary School, Borden

The Maid

Once upon a time, there was a maid, her name was Miss Drury. She worked hard. The prince made an announcement, he said that he was looking for a bride that was a princess. He looked everywhere but he couldn't find one. The maid's stepmom and stepsister heard that and pretended to be princesses. Miss Drury went and said that she was a princess, they used a lie detector on her, Miss Drury was telling the truth. A few days later, she got married to the prince and lived happily ever after.

Zikra Lal (8)
Cravenwood Primary Academy, Crumpsall

Wild Life

Once upon a time, I was wandering in the woods with my sister. We saw a snake and got scared. We ran and saw a squirrel and some beautiful butterflies. We also heard different sounds of birds, we saw some bugs flying around us. I saw an owl sitting on a tree. I enjoyed myself a lot in the woods. I picked some sticks. It was getting dark so we went home and decided to go back again the next morning. It was so much fun. I hope to see a monkey and deer or a tiger next time.

Khadija Irfan (7)
Cravenwood Primary Academy, Crumpsall

The Police Agency

It was getting dark, so Isla decided to head to the secret meeting spot. Her best friends were there, discussing something. Isla joined in. They were talking about finding an escaped prisoner. "This is the best job ever," proclaimed Isla. All her friends agreed, so they decided to have a party to celebrate. Isla brought all the decorations and then set them up. But just as the party was starting, they got a phone call. There was another escaped prisoner on the loose. "Where should we start?" asked Isla.
"We'll start at the prisoner hideout," said her best friend Timmy.

Piper Kirkwood-Wilson (8)
Eccleston St Mary's CE Primary School, Eccleston

The Boy And The Creatures

Once upon a time, a boy walked straight through a portal into a clearing in the woods. In the clearing stood two dogs, a lion, a gorilla, a dinosaur and a cross between an eagle and a lion. All of them were stood around a tree with a wand, shining in the sun, leaning against the tree. The boy walked forward and said, "Hello, I'm Boy." The creatures all moved so that he could get to the tree.
A voice suddenly said, "Forget your cruel life, you're one of us now," and they lived happily ever after.

Daniel Traynor (8)
Eccleston St Mary's CE Primary School, Eccleston

Timmy And The Magic Portal

Once upon a time, a boy called Timmy was walking down a scary street. In front of him was a strange, mysterious portal. Cautiously, he crept inside and saw a complicated maze in front of him. It was creepy, scary and dark, with strange things hanging above him. He went left, right, forwards and backwards to find his way through. But then, Timmy could see a bright, glaring light and he knew he was nearly out. Then, he heard footsteps behind him. He started to panic, his heart raced wildly, so he ran like a bullet out of there...

Leo Berto (8)
Eccleston St Mary's CE Primary School, Eccleston

A Wander In The Woods

Once upon a time, there were two boys, called Timmy and Bob. They were playing football and Bob kicked the ball into the forest and they heard a voice coming from inside the woods shouting, "Ouch!" The boys went to look. As they got closer, they could see two big eyes staring at them, and a big mouth with their ball stuck in it. The tree was alive! The boys had to tickle under its branches and poke its nose until he spat their ball out of its mouth. Timmy and Bob snatched the ball and quickly ran away.

Theo Wright (8)
Eccleston St Mary's CE Primary School, Eccleston

A Wander In The Woods

Once upon a time, there was a young girl called Scarlett, who liked to wander in the woods behind her house. One day, whilst walking, Scarlett stumbled upon a magic portal between some bushes and jumped into it and landed in a secret fairyland where she met a unicorn called Miss Shine. Miss Shine granted her three wishes, her first wish was for a pet dog, her second wish was a big chocolate cake and her third wish was to get back home to her mum and dad and see if her wishes came true and they really had done.

Grace Aspinall (8)
Eccleston St Mary's CE Primary School, Eccleston

The Abandoned School

Once, there was a boy called Timmy who went into an abandoned forest. In the distance, he saw a missing cat, Timmy kept it. A few moments later, they saw an abandoned school, they went in. Inside was a door, they opened it. Behind was a monster! Timmy ran as fast as he could. Timmy and his cat were looking behind them so without noticing ran into a portal. The monster stopped, luckily the portal led Timmy home. Timmy decided to keep the cat forever, he named him Whiskers.

Jacob Redgrave (8)
Eccleston St Mary's CE Primary School, Eccleston

Escaping Dr Man

They had escaped! Dr Man had locked them there for a year now. Sam saw two dark figures, "Who are you?" he said.
"I'm Louise," said one.
"I'm John," said the other.
"Where are we?" asked Sam.
"That is the question," replied John.
"Argh!" screamed Louise.
They both turned around screaming her name which they had just learned.
"Louise," they screamed. Where did she go and how was she going to get back?
"This has something to do with Dr Man," said John.
"Well that's obvious," said Sam, and they set off...

Oscar Atkinson (8)
ESMS Junior School, Edinburgh

The Dark Lord

I'd escaped the evil king. I was about to celebrate but something rattled in the bushes. An investigation was needed. I looked for hours but nothing, then I heard it again. What could it be? Suddenly, it revealed itself. It was a crow lying before my eyes, I helped it. Then it spoke, "The Dark Lord has sent scouts to find you, return to your village!" So I went to my village to find it was burnt. The Dark Lord had found it. This was perfect for setting up a camp at least. Ekko, my dog, survived the Dark Lord.

Matthew Goodbrand (9)
ESMS Junior School, Edinburgh

The Night Of The Jokers

Once upon a time, I heard the doorbell ring and when I opened the door a creepy joker was there. He threw a piece of paper and vanished in a puff of smoke. I magically appeared in a dark cave where three jokers looked exactly the same. They were standing in front of me. The door locked. "If you get out, we won't kill you," said the jokers. Wait, where did they go? I saw a slide, I went down it and saw an entrance to freedom, but where was I? The jokers were there, they vanished into smoke.

Giselle Lee (9)
ESMS Junior School, Edinburgh

The Creepy Noise

One dark and spooky night, I was tiptoeing along a bumpy path. Something was making an unusual noise behind me. Suddenly, I jumped in surprise. It was just a baby fox. I named it Ginger. In the misty distance, I could just see a rusty door. I tried to open it but it was stuck. I spotted something hidden next to a toadstool. I wandered over to it. This was the luckiest thing. It was a key. I slowly opened the door with the silver key. Inside was a beautiful chest. I opened it and there was a magic ring.

Amber Cattanach (8)
ESMS Junior School, Edinburgh

A Lush Green Forest...

Once upon a time, I found a beautiful wood. It had lush green trees, oh the lush green trees! I chose to have a wander so I went in. What I didn't know was that this forest had horror! I was now getting closer to the centre of the forest but now I was scared. Just then, an ice dragon landed into my clearing and said in her cold voice, "I will take you home." I climbed onto the dragon called Everesta's back and we flew. The sky was amazing, Everesta put me down and I rushed home.

Laila Dewar (8)
ESMS Junior School, Edinburgh

The Toadstool

Once there was a toadstool and inside it there were fairies. One was called Poppy and another was called Pippa. All day long they would play, and every time a person went past they would fly up a tree or fly to the toadstool. They would play tig and hide-and-seek, they found it so fun. The toadstool had red glitter on it - apart from that it was normal. Unfortunately, one day, a person found the fairies and took them away. The toadstool was empty for the rest of its time. Where did they go?

Erin O'Brien (9)
ESMS Junior School, Edinburgh

The Hidden World

One dark night, I explored the forest. I always wanted to see it. Suddenly, at the end of the forest, a mist appeared. I went deeper in and then out of nowhere there was a huge cave. I went into the cave but then the entrance closed! There must be a way out. Then I had an idea, there must be an exit. But instead of finding the exit, I went deeper in the cave. I kept going until I saw the end of the cave. I had found a hidden world. Suddenly, a monster appeared! The monster killed me.

Junming Che (8)
ESMS Junior School, Edinburgh

The Flush Of Water

I arrived at the meeting place and we talked for a while about who had killed the chief. It was getting dark but as I was leaving they slammed the door and water started seeping through the walls. There must be a way out, otherwise, the men in the room would still be here. I heard a noise behind me and I saw the men escaping through a sliding wall. I leapt for it. I made it through the wall but when I looked down I was falling to the ground. Now I know who killed the chief.

Sophie Seddon (9)
ESMS Junior School, Edinburgh

Camping Deep, Deep In The Woods

Once upon a time, in the woods, there was a boy camping with his friends deep in the forest. One night, he woke up in his tent to hear a very scary noise. He didn't know what it was so he went back to sleep. Five minutes later, he heard it again so this time he went out into the dark forest and he saw something in the trees. He was now terrified. He wanted to go back. The next morning, his friends woke up to find their friend was gone. They looked for him with no luck.

Roddy Browne (9)
ESMS Junior School, Edinburgh

The Creepy Mist

Once upon a time, there was a creepy mist and I could not see anything so then I followed the mist to see where it was coming from. The next moment I was there. I found an abandoned house so bravely I went in. All of a sudden, the door slammed. And then I heard a noise behind me. Shocked, I saw a strange-looking monster. Amazed, I rubbed my eyes but it was just a dream. Quickly, I went to tell my mum but she was sleeping. I then looked outside, the mist was there!

Lily Paulo (8)
ESMS Junior School, Edinburgh

The Night Walker

This morning I woke up with blood on my neck. I was a bit confused but I ignored it. At school I felt a bit dizzy and light-headed, then I fainted. I woke up at the same spot so I went home and went to sleep. This time when I woke up it was 3am and I felt a bit bloodthirsty and there was a knife in my hand. At that moment, I felt strange so I went for a walk. I walked about a mile then I walked home. Luckily it was just a dream, phew!

Johnny Forbes (9)
ESMS Junior School, Edinburgh

Through The Forest...

One dark, winter evening, I was walking through a mythical forest. Suddenly, I came to a stop. Everything was silent. No robins were chirping and no trees were swaying. I felt petrified but soon after that moment, I was lifted away by a gust of wind. Soon after a minute had gone by, I was in a room with flickering lights and screechy doors. Oh wait, it was just a nightmare. The next day I told Mum and Dad all about it.

Lucy Gammell (9)
ESMS Junior School, Edinburgh

The Thunder Troopers

It was getting dark, Solo, Yoda and Leia arrived in the woods. They walked back to their base through dark woods. The night was cold, there was frost forming on the branches. Leia heard animals scurrying through the undergrowth, cracking of twigs underfoot was heard ahead of them. Suddenly they looked up and saw many eyes peering out of the darkness. Who was there? The Thunder Troopers had them surrounded. Slowly, the eyes moved forward. There was no chance of escape. The Thunder Troopers immediately threw down a net, capturing Solo and his friends, will they survive?

Ross Bailey (11)
Friars Academy, Wellingborough

Dave's Shepherd's Pie

Once upon a time, there was a man called Dave, he made shepherd's pie for the clowns to use in their show. One day, he went into the woods. Dave got lost, he did not know what to do but he had a shepherd's pie, so Dave went to sleep.

In the morning, Dave looked for his shepherd's pie and then *wwham!* He looked down and it was his shepherd's pie. Dave was scared but then the shepherd's pie said, "Don't eat me, I taste good but I don't want to be eaten please." Dave was scared and ran away.

Katie Jones (12)
Friars Academy, Wellingborough

The Rabbit Attacks

There must be a way out, The gate was locked. I started running. I heard its paws behind me. I zoomed into an abandoned cage, it smelt horrible. Bouncing around, I heard it on the cage roof. Holding my breath, it came in, I crawled out unwittingly. I went into the vents. No one was in there, I swooped out and saw the bunny. It seemed like it was running in circles. Luckily, there were some tools to escape. I started grabbing the tools. The bunny could sense me escaping. I started banging the lock with the tools, *bang bang.*

Ben Lawrence (12)
Friars Academy, Wellingborough

The Nice Witch

Once, there were three children, the kids were called Sofia, Fredy and Jeanette. In the morning, they got kicked out by their parents and got lost. At night, they walked and walked. They saw pink, glowing smoke. They followed it and saw an edible place. A house made out of gingerbread, where a kind witch lived. She wasn't mean, not ugly and did not eat children like other witches. She let the three kids stay, they had food, a nice bed and toys to play with. They called the kind witch Mother, they were now a perfect family.

Sienna Edwards (12)
Friars Academy, Wellingborough

The Bunker

Sam and Joe were in the woods. Suddenly, Sam tripped and fell onto a door. Sam looked down and got up. He opened the door. Joe went down in the dark with Sam. It took them a few minutes to see in the dark. It was smelly and dirty. They saw a creepy door. Joe opened it, there was a chest. They opened the oak chest. It was full of gold and silver. They took the chest home and went upstairs to Joe's bedroom and emptied the chest. The next thing they took the gold and silver to be sold.

Alex Adair (12)
Friars Academy, Wellingborough

The Magical Chocolate House

Once there was a girl named Emily and her friend, they were walking through the woods looking for food then suddenly they saw a chocolate house. Oh my goodness it was magnificent. Then a young man came out of the house, the children crept up to the house and tasted it without anyone noticing. As the children munched on the chocolate house they grew fatter and fatter, they felt scared and panicked, the house was magical and sparkling. They both didn't feel well and went home to bed.

Cordell Thomas (12)
Friars Academy, Wellingborough

Into The Woods With The Bears

In the distance, I saw a baby bear. I went closer. The bear looked scared as it curled into itself. I slowly moved up to the bear and stroked its back to calm it. I looked at its leg, it was broken. I pulled out my first-aid kit and bandaged the leg. Slowly, the bear started to walk and followed me. I heard in the distance a mamma bear calling her cub. I heard twigs cracking. I started to get scared. Suddenly, a big, wet nose came up behind me and put me on the ground.

Bradley Smith (11)
Friars Academy, Wellingborough

The Monster In The Woods

Once upon a time, I just went to take a walk in the woods. It was only me and no one else. I felt like there was nothing there. After about half an hour I walked over a hill. I heard a noise, I looked over. Right in front of me, there was a giant monster with a giant, shiny, silver axe. I screamed and ran for my life. I was so scared. I didn't look behind me. I heard his footsteps behind me. He caught up with me and picked me up but he seemed to be friendly.

Stanley Martyne (12)
Friars Academy, Wellingborough

The Mystery Of The Vampire Girl

On a full moon, a compassionate, introverted girl was camping. It was a sombre atmosphere and she woke up. From nowhere, a shimmering portal appeared. With naivety, she obtained courage and stepped in. It came to her senses that it was a vampire world! She was adapting to the new environment but discovered someone called Dracula, who was treating everybody carelessly. Ashley finally attained confidence and slew Dracula once and for all. But then she realised something; she was only hallucinating from camping since she didn't even want to go. Her heart was pounding hastily and she finally woke up.

Grace Kwarteng (10)
Grove Primary School, Wolverhampton

Beyond The Gate

Once upon a time, I was in a forest walking all alone. I was calm until I saw a gate... I hadn't seen that gate before in the forest. I encouraged myself and opened the gate and entered the mysterious place. I saw blue light, glimmering butterflies, marvellous flowers and I saw fairies for the first time. The fairies asked me who I was and I answered them by saying my name. Me and the fairies became close friends. Sometime later, a monster appeared in front of me. They saved me and I returned home without telling anyone what happened.

Simran Kaur Gill (11)
Grove Primary School, Wolverhampton

The Secret Meeting Place

Once upon a time, I escaped from home. I walked for more than twenty-five minutes, I arrived at the secret place, it was really dark and scary. I heard a deep, creepy voice behind me. I was getting scared, I looked behind me but there was nothing behind me. I thought I was imagining but I wasn't. It was getting creepy. I heard someone saying, "Hello, I'm here." I wanted to go back home but I forgot the way out. I had to sleep in my car. I couldn't sleep at all. I finally escaped the secret meeting place.

Almaza
Grove Primary School, Wolverhampton

Caged

It was getting dark so I had to take the shortcut home... The woods. I walked about fifteen feet into the forest and I heard something above me. Suddenly, a dome made out of sticks fell on top of me. What do I do? I threw rocks at the sticks and tried to kick my way through, it was not working. Then I saw bright red eyes through the shadows. Now, I was panicking. I couldn't break through and there was a monster in the shadows. Then it rapidly crawled at me, the last trace of me was my scream.

Louie Fellows (9)
Grove Primary School, Wolverhampton

The Blood Bender

The moon was at its fullest, the sky at its darkest. TJ was playing football in a playground next to a dark forest. TJ and his friends were just playing. Suddenly, Rob kicked the ball into the forest. This forest was known for a person called the Blood Bender. The Blood Bender could control anyone.
"What can we do?" said Rob, with sweat running down his face.
"We'll all go in," said Tulsi, feeling fearless.
They stepped into the forest, they saw a dark figure in the distance, it moved towards them. They ran, but it was too late, *crunch!*

Archie Brooksbank (11)
Headlands Primary School, Northampton

Little Red Riding Wolf

Walking through the woods, a figure emerged from a distance, a girl who was neatly costumed like a wolf approached a group of lovely pigs who were minding their own business. The pigs looked in disbelief. Used to the wolves visiting, one pig cried, "We told you not to visit again!"

The pretend wolf, who was confused and lost, held out a basket of fresh apples.

"Why should we trust you?" laughed another pig.

The wolf became silent, stepping back as the girl took off her costume. The pigs felt mistaken when they found out she was not the wolf.

Kassie Teeboon (11)
Headlands Primary School, Northampton

Hunted

Not long ago, I escaped. I'm hiding behind a gravestone, hiding from the mysterious man. He is tall, about six feet with red, glowing eyes. Fearing for my life, I tiptoe slowly to the foggy, forgotten forest, snapping the small sticks. My heart is beating, my head is sweating, my hands are shaking. I'm lost, what do I do? What if he finds me? What if he kills me? No, I'm overreacting. "Lola, stop scaring yourself," I say, but then I hear a voice, a high voice, a high calming voice... "Wow, what a good book," I murmur.

Lola Claringbold (11)
Headlands Primary School, Northampton

The Girl Who Turns Into A Bear

Thump! Yanka opens her eyes. She wakes up to see brown walnut bear legs. Rubs her eyes to make sure she's not dreaming. The last thing she remembers is falling off a hill. Whilst Yanka is in her room she can hear the leaves saying, "Yanka, come here." It makes her very curious and she really wants to know what's in the magical forest. That night, she left her village and wandered into the woods. She saw big bears, wonderful wolves, brown owls and a bunny hopping around. As she got deeper into the woods she turned into a bear...

Jovanna Jojo (11)
Headlands Primary School, Northampton

The Shadow Man

I escaped the cell. I stepped onto the luscious ground. Suddenly, memories came back to me. Sneakily, I was roaming the forest to find a hiding spot. I went towards the bush, making sure I was covered. *Bang!* Darkness all over me. Now I was here. Picking up the pace, I began to leave. Suddenly, I heard a voice and ran towards it. When I arrived something was off. The air turned from sweet aromas to disgusting stenches. Suddenly, a figure chased me. I ran away. I was bolting through the forest, twisting and turning until finally, I found home.

Greta Meskauskaite (11)
Headlands Primary School, Northampton

The Spooky Door

Crack, a branch snapped. Ella and Noah kept walking as terror stared into their souls. In the distance, a red, dripping door, slowly opening, the door squeaked. Ella and Noah stepped through the door. Suddenly, *bang!* The door shut, then screams echoed through the maze. Instantly, clowns ran around the corner, bats flew from the roof. "There must be a way out of here," shouted Noah. All of a sudden, the bright red door appeared.
"Quickly," shouted Ella, as Ella and Noah ran as fast as lightning to the door.

Aoife Collins (11)
Headlands Primary School, Northampton

The Killing Truth

One gloomy, dark, dangerous night, me and my friends Jessi and Tye went out at midnight. "Did you hear that?" I asked silently.
"No," they both whispered.
Suddenly, something pushed so hard onto the floor, we could hardly breathe. A couple of minutes later we got up but when we got up Jessi was gone. When we looked down blood was lying right where Jessi was lying. We followed the trail of blood. It led us to an abandoned house. "Shall we go in?" Tye asked.
"Yes," I said.
The search began.

Amy Heath (11)
Headlands Primary School, Northampton

The Lost Doll

In the dark, I was on a walk. Then, rabbits were hopping towards me. They suddenly started biting my leg; it was like they wanted me to follow them. So I followed them. They led me to a house that said, 'If you enter, you won't return'. My heart stopped. I went in and looked around. Minutes later, I saw a doll with red eyes. I laughed and then turned around but then something grabbed my leg. I wanted to run. I couldn't move. The doll said, "Who's laughing now? You're never going back, you're going to die!"

Sara Sultan (11)
Headlands Primary School, Northampton

Back From The Dead

As usual, me and my twin sister Maisie went to play hide-and-seek in the woods. When we were playing we found a door, a huge, brown, dusty door. We entered, all our brother's things were all over the floor. It was dark. Red, deathly blood was all up the walls. His name was Ray, he went missing four years ago. We stepped in closer and Maisie screamed. Someone grabbed us. It was Ray. The door shut. "Hello again," he said in a sinister voice. "I have been waiting for you." He pushed me to the floor. Maisie was gone...

Lily Owen (11)
Headlands Primary School, Northampton

I Want To Help

There must be a way out. I had to get out of there. Then suddenly, I heard footsteps coming near me. *Click!* The door handle clicked. *Creak!* The door opened. My heart was pounding, I was begging that it wasn't my stepdad. It was! There he was, standing in front of me. "Don't come near me!" I shouted. He started to walk near me.
"I want to help you," he said softly.
"What with? You will never help me!" I cried.
"I want to help you find your mum," he smirked...

Irina Bilali (10)
Headlands Primary School, Northampton

Mysterious Woods

In the middle of the night, I found myself in a forest. I didn't know how I got there. It was mysterious and eerie. I needed to get home. A harrowing, spine-chilling caw sound weaved through the gnarled, withering trees like strangling string. A cold mist covered the forest like a mask. As quiet as a mouse, I darted, occasionally crunching twigs. My heart pounded, hammering on my ribs. I ran so hard my legs felt like jelly. The moon shone a pearly white aura. I was out. Finally! *Crunch*, something was close behind me...

Imran Ahmed (11)
Headlands Primary School, Northampton

The Girl Who Speaks Bear

Crash! All of the trees in the forest had collapsed. I heard a noise. It was a mysterious, creepy noise. There it was again. I looked around the forest in fear. Then I saw some hazelnut-brown eyes in the emerald-green bushes. It jumped out of the bushes with a loud heinous roar. It was a bear! I said to myself, "Be calm, it's only a bear." So I calmed myself down and started slowly walking to the bear, it was gigantic. The bear started to speak in bear language, I realised I could speak 'bear' too.

Brackyn Joseph (11)
Headlands Primary School, Northampton

Chased

I heard a noise behind me. Legs shivering, palms sweating. "Get him!" a deep voice behind me shouted. I was frozen until I felt hands on my back. Suddenly, I fell. I looked up, it was a boy. "Who are you?" I questioned, no answer. I leapt on my feet, brushing myself down. "I have to deliver something." I ran as quick as possible towards the delivery point. Tall trees surrounded me. I turned around, the boy still following me. There was a large cliff, I had to jump. "I can't do it..."

Max Knight (11)
Headlands Primary School, Northampton

The Way Home

I escaped. The ebony cage hung from the caramel tree. My hands were sore from the interlocking chains. I stepped into the soft ground, lost in the wildlife. I bolted across the forest, knowing where to go. In the distance, I saw a campfire. Lying my head on one of the logs, I drifted to sleep.
Waking up, the rays of the sun shone through. I sat up, rubbing my eyes. Standing up, I continued home. Making my way through the forest, I pushed the branches and leaves, in the distance, I saw a village. I bolted through. Home...

Austin Seby (11)
Headlands Primary School, Northampton

A Place I Called Home

As I trundled through the forest, my legs trembled, fresh sweat rolled down my cheek. I wanted to turn back but I couldn't. The place I had run from. The place I called home. The wind was so shrill as it whistled around my ears. Branches clawed at my clothes. My feet ached, my head pounded. I journeyed on, trying not to think about the pain. My breath was hemmed inside me as I saw a silhouette looming in the distance. Then I realised it wasn't in the distance, it was coming closer and closer. I froze, then ran...

Faith Preston-Nel (11)
Headlands Primary School, Northampton

The Trip

Late at night, Fred, Katy and Amy went camping. No one was around. They set up their tent. Amy suggested to go and collect sticks for the campfire. Amy was in the woods, collecting sticks, Amy was pinned to a tree, a gun pointed to her head. *Boom!* The gunshot, then Fred and Katy appeared. Amy was safe but the man got away. It didn't mean he wouldn't come back. They went back to the campsite but Amy was still worried about that man who tried to kill her. Someone was outside of her tent, but who was it?

Ruby Skelton (11)
Headlands Primary School, Northampton

The Girl Who Met A Bear

I was nervous. But why was I nervous? Maybe because I was surrounded by darkness, maybe because it was past midnight or maybe because I could hear rustling coming from the bush behind me. I didn't know? I grabbed my flashlight out of my backpack and set off on my nightly journey. I walked through the bushes. I walked through the puddles and the bushes. I walked through towering trees, puddles and bushes. Suddenly, I saw something fluffy, a pillow? No, it was a bear, I was scared, but it wanted to be friends!

Emily Owen (11)
Headlands Primary School, Northampton

The Diamond

Running through the woods, I stopped. I had found it. I touched the stone. With the sharp edges pricking me. Slowly, I reached out my bony hands and took the jewel, glinting in the moonlight. Suddenly, they appeared behind me and as quick as a flash, they raced towards me, anger in their eyes, I was taken away. They locked me up but forgot to take away the diamond in their haste. As soon as they were gone, I opened the window with my sword and escaped. I ran back to the woods and found the portal, I was free.

Kaysah Rahman (11)
Headlands Primary School, Northampton

The Treasure

I made it to the island where the treasure was supposed to be. I searched for hours. Oh yeah, my name is Ellie and my friend's name is Daniel. He stayed home today.
Five hours later, I finally found the lost treasure and I called my friend to come. Night-time came and my friend arrived. Two hours later, we saw a dark figure. He had deep red eyes and was really tall. He disappeared. We then went home and ever since then I've seen him in the corner of my room staring at me every single night.

Evie Wilson (10)
Headlands Primary School, Northampton

The Kidnap

I escaped from Alcatraz prison. Running for my life, I outpaced the police, jumped into an old door and was teleported to an enchanted forest. Three years later, I'm the king of a village and warrior.
One day when me and my troop were out running, someone kidnapped our village elders. We searched for them. We arrived at a rival village. The elders were hanging from their feet, facing down at hot lava. I fought them all off, *shing, shang, pow!* I rescued them all and we had a huge party.

Jay Evans
Headlands Primary School, Northampton

The Wolf Tale

Midnight struck, I was walking in the woods with my brother, behind us there was a noise. There was a dark figure hiding behind a caramel-brown tree, it was a man. He was holding a gun. I told my brother and we ran. The hunter realised and followed. We lost him. We ran up a hill where the moon shone brightly. My brother was panting, begging for water. I said to myself, "We didn't deserve this, why is this happening to us?" We went home and told Mum. Then gunshots. The hunter was back...

Evie Hamilton-Atkins (10)
Headlands Primary School, Northampton

The Duel

Leo stopped as a man appeared. The man had a white beard down to his feet and red eyes. He raised his wand and so did Leo. Then as quick as a flash, a beam of immense power erupted from their wands. Their beams met in the middle of the clearing and a force pushed them both into trees. Leo looked up and there was the man, standing above him, foot on chest, he aimed his wand, shot. Leo ducked and the tree fell on the man. Leo ran and thought he would never see him again, but he would...

Leo Hammond-Wood (10)
Headlands Primary School, Northampton

The Detective

This is the story about a man named John Parklif. He was a very good detective and solved all of his cases. On one specific case, there was a catastrophic event that got him fired and ruined his whole career.

One dull day, he went to work and started to study the victims. A gun was left behind by the killer so John did some fingerprint tests. At his lab, he did the fingerprint tests and stood there as white as a ghost. The screen said 'fingerprint owner... John Parklif'.

Kian Mcgee (10)
Headlands Primary School, Northampton

Lost In The Woods

As it was still light, I decided to go for a walk like I usually do. I wanted to take a different route, I went through the woods. As I started to walk towards the woods, the night started to fall. It got darker. I started to feel scared and suddenly I was kidnapped. I couldn't see anything. I could make out a figure holding a gun to my head. I didn't know if I would survive? There was a man watching me, he fell asleep so I managed to grab the keys and run for my life.

Skye England (11)
Headlands Primary School, Northampton

The Missing Boy

I once woke up in a forest, still in my bed, but it was covered in moss. I got out of it and went to explore. The trees had no lower branches to climb. There was some kind of mist and vines everywhere and deer screamed in the distance, I thought there were wolves in the woods. Then behind me a twig snapped and out came the creature, at first I thought it was a man until I saw the face. The face was star shape with a dark hole in the middle and teeth on each side, with blood...

Keelan Crouch (11)
Headlands Primary School, Northampton

The Dark Night

I stood there, quiet and still. My voice slowly stuttered in horror. The ebony, jade and obsidian night made me lose all vision. My memory came back to me. I remember lying peacefully in my bed until I heard a knock on my front door and then, *bang!* I was on the floor. I was in the pitch-black. I slowly tiptoed forward. My eyes watered in joy and horror. Sitting on a slate, charcoal bench was my dad. "Dad!" I shouted. He didn't reply, he just stared...

Yohan Aneesh (10)
Headlands Primary School, Northampton

Haunted House

My family moved to a haunted house in Mushroom Valley. The doorknob was ready to fall off. I opened the door, the light was flickering. I heard footsteps run and sprint across the landing. A vase fell. I heard screaming. I ran upstairs, blood was spewed across the hallway. I ran downstairs. My dad was gone. I opened the door to the hallway exit, it was locked. I screamed. A shadow came towards me. I woke up in a forest. I was covered in blood. "Did I kill them?"

Scarlett Handley (11)
Headlands Primary School, Northampton

The Shadow

In the distance, I saw a tall, ebony shadow. "Why are you running, little man?" said the man with a raucous voice. As bats and birds hung around a tree, darkness came. Without a single breath, he ran towards me. I fell. It was getting dark. Around the corner, I glared at glowing treasure. I went. I opened it, there was a key inside. There was a building in the woods, I ran towards it. The man was getting faster, *boom.* I opened the door, he caught me...

Elwin Joy (11)
Headlands Primary School, Northampton

The Girl

Years ago, there was a girl called 'The Girl'. Her parents died when she was at a young age and she always got made fun of and bullied a lot for it. As she grew older she started to kill and kidnap. She usually kidnapped and killed five to a thousand people a day. It depended on how she was feeling. You're maybe wondering how she could kill so many people, well she had a special technique.
One day, she was walking and the unbelievable happened...

Ruby Stewart (11)
Headlands Primary School, Northampton

Kidnapped!

As the old man blew out the fire, there was a *bang!* The old man was walking across to investigate, he disappeared. Police came, they were baffled as there were no traces. The investigation crew had no evidence of kidnapping but they saw a phone. It was the old man's phone, there were footprints leading to a cottage. Police pulled their tasers out and knocked on the door, a woman came out, they saw the old man, they rescued him and arrested the woman.

Omid Rasuli (10)
Headlands Primary School, Northampton

A Mystery Place

Hi! My name is Kelsey and my friend's name is Evie. Me and Evie were going to an abandoned hospital in London. It was going to be fun and we were taking a Ouji board to talk to spirits. I started driving and then we saw the hospital. It was so disgusting and dirty. We were walking up to the door and a figure ran past. We jumped and were anxious. We went inside and a creepy young doll jumped at me and Evie. We were so scared. We both left.

Kelsey Windram (11)
Headlands Primary School, Northampton

The Beast In The Woods

I was in the woods playing and then I saw a strange door. I walked over and opened it. It was a blue portal. I went in and then I walked out the door into a strange land. A beast came and tried to kill me and I hid behind a wall until it left. I just ran until I stopped. It was so nice here, I wish I could stay here. I just walked around until I saw the beast again I ran in the opposite direction, I saw a portal and ran through, back home.

Mia Carter (10)
Headlands Primary School, Northampton

The Secret Door

In the distance, I saw a shimmering golden glow. The glow was so bright I couldn't look at it for much longer. I wondered what it was. Nervously, I crept forward. Now I could see that the glow was a fairy. I gasped in shock. Suddenly, the beautiful fairy saw me. Quickly, she sprinted off into the dark woods. I chased her, my heart pounding like a drum. Eventually, the fairy jumped to the top of an ancient oak tree. I followed her through an ornate door, the other side was truly magical. "I wonder what adventures I will have..."

Alessia de Molfetta-Page (10)
Holy Family Catholic Primary School, Ingol

That Little Wolf

One bright sunny morning, I went for a little stroll in the woods. "Nature is so pretty!" I exclaimed. Kneeling down to get a pretty picture I heard the bush rustling behind me. I turned around and I saw two little beady eyes. I jumped, "Argh! What was that?!" I exclaimed. I pulled back the bush and you wouldn't believe what I saw, it was a wolf pup. "Aww," I said. "You must be lost, let's take you back to your mother." The pup guided me to his home from his smell.

Myla Spencer (10)
Holy Family Catholic Primary School, Ingol

Secret Place

Finally, I arrived at the secret place which was a castle. At first, I thought it was the wrong address but it was the correct one. There was a laboratory room. I looked over in the castle, it was my old friend from school. I was very surprised so we walked together until the professor came. It was the most aggressive professor in the world, when you say something wrong he kicks you out! But the professor went a different way, we went to head and asked could we have a new professor, she said yes.

Lena Siatka (10)
Holy Family Catholic Primary School, Ingol

Scary Night

It was getting dark, I was going to sleep in my bed and quickly fell asleep. Then a few hours later I woke up in the middle of the night. I was so scared because I saw a big, scary vampire. He had lots of blood on his large, sharp teeth. Around me, it was so frightening. I was panicking and began to cry. I carefully went downstairs, but there was no one. But it was just one of my stupid dreams. In the morning there were no more frightening or scary things.

Klara Barbara Buczkowska (10)
Holy Family Catholic Primary School, Ingol

Walking In The Woods

In the distance, I saw wolves, but we scared them away. We were walking in the woods, we saw trees of green and dark insects. The ground was wet. We were now going back to our campervan to eat. We heard the wolves, far away. We were scared. A bear came but ran away from us. As we went back outside we saw a squirrel. There was a bush with berries on it, we picked them all and we washed them and ate them. It got dark and we had to go to sleep.

Olivia Fryzowska (9)
Holy Family Catholic Primary School, Ingol

Trapped

I am scared, I can't escape, it is like an endless loop. My name is Evan and I'm wandering in the woods and I've never been so scared. If you see this, send help, I'm gonna try and escape, wait, what was that? It was some sort of monster, it looked like a big dog. I'm gonna investigate. Hmm. I can't find it, wait, there it is, I have to run as fast as I can. If you see this, help me.

Jack Fletcher (10)
Holy Family Catholic Primary School, Ingol

Magic Frog

I'd escaped, there was a frog. The wind blowing had me even more terrified. I ran and ran but it caught up to me. The frog must have had magical powers and it controlled my brain. He told me a secret message that I was scared to listen to, he said that there was a way out, he could only show it in my brain, so I followed the path and escaped.

Olivia Rudzka (10)
Holy Family Catholic Primary School, Ingol

The Legendary Ice Dragon

I heard a noise behind me, I turned around and saw the legendary Ice Dragon. I'm going to tell you how I got here. I'm Alexina, I was going today to the woods after I saw the dragon's den, I peeked in and nothing so I went inside and saw the ancient death sword. I took it. When I went outside and saw the legendary Ice Dragon, I took out my sword and killed it. The dragon perished. Then I saw a dragon egg. If I hatched it, it could be my pet.

Varswati Das (10)
King Solomon International Business School, Birmingham

Unknown

As it was getting dark, I was wandering through the woods and my phone rang. It was an unknown number. I didn't answer but kept walking. I heard a crunch behind me but nothing was there. I checked my phone, it was on zero percent battery. The last time I checked it, it was on one hundred percent. I freaked out, my heart was trying to escape, my eyes were popping out and my legs couldn't hold my weight. Out of nowhere, random voices were stuck in my head, but then everything instantly stopped and everything was silent...

Ulde Burleviciute (10)
Lakeside Primary Academy, Frimley

Wolf Attack

It was getting dark, my mum called me in for dinner. Accidentally, the ball went over the tree so I went to collect it. Inside the mysterious woods, I found my ball. As I was heading back I heard a snap and a howl. I started running. Strangely, I could no longer hear anything. I calmed down. Suddenly, something leapt at me and bit my finger off. I fainted. I woke up in a house full of pictures of wolves. I couldn't move. Unexpectedly, a wolf came into the room. As I was about to scream, the wolf started talking...

Jayden Duffin (10)
Lakeside Primary Academy, Frimley

Danger In The Woods

It was getting dark and cold. I had spent two days in the woods. It was such a dumb idea to run away from my parents. I had eaten nothing and was becoming weaker. My mum would have paid the police to come and search for me by now. Suddenly, I heard snapping slowly coming towards me. I looked back and saw a hooded shadow with a knife covered in blood and a poster of me saying, 'Dead or alive, reward, £200,000'. I started to run but he grabbed onto my foot and dragged me to the ground...

Noah Brown (10)
Lakeside Primary Academy, Frimley

The Zombies

While it was getting dark, my mum called me on my phone as I had been outside all day with my best friend Jakob. So I started to run back home. All of a sudden, I fell over. Then I got up from the ground. I saw some hideous, gruesome zombies dancing to a song, I tried to keep as quiet as a mouse. As quick as a flash, I started to sprint away but I stepped on a broken twig and all of a sudden the zombies stared at me, I screamed!

Jake Seward (10)
Lakeside Primary Academy, Frimley

A Scare In The Woods

It was getting dark and Katy was stuck in the woods, she had got lost in the woods and soon it got dark and she started to hear noises, Katy heard bats and wolves. She started to cry and walked home but ended up walking in circles. It turned out it was Katy's friend, Lucy, making those noises because they made a bet that Lucy couldn't scare Katy, Katy had now lost the bet. Lucy felt bad because she had scared Katy so much she decided to explain the whole story, Lucy knew the way home and they walked together.

Darcie Dunbar (9)
Lenham Primary School, Lenham

Zombie Attack

It was getting dark when me and my friend Bob were in the treehouse. We heard a noise. I asked, "What was that?" Outside was a blood-sucking zombie. I quickly grabbed the key and ran to the door to lock the door fast. We were frightened for our lives, we could not go to sleep. We waited and got bored but then we heard an almighty bang! It was the zombie trying to break down the door. The scary zombie eventually made a hole through the door, we were terrified and couldn't think of anything to do...

Oliver Watson (10)
Ling Bob JI&N School, Pellon

A Scary Camp Trip

It was getting dark, so me and my friends, Thea, Phoebe and Chloe were going to roast some marshmallows over the campfire. We told some ghost stories but we thought one of them actually came to life. After we had gone to sleep in the tent, we woke up to the scariest sound known to mankind. We all ran into one room of the tent because the tent was massive and split into four rooms and, scared for our lives, we all hid under the duvet in Thea's room and then we heard the zip go...

Megan Watson (11)
Ling Bob JI&N School, Pellon

A Surprising Encounter

On a gloomy, rainy Saturday, I was sitting on a metal park bench in New York. Suddenly, I spotted a shiny purple apple next to me. Surprised, I picked it up, biting into the juicy pulp. Munching away, I realised a green, thin, soulless worm was staring into my eyes, "We've been trying to contact you."
"What are you talking about? Am I hallucinating?"
"We have been attempting to contact you regarding your car's extended warranty," smiled the worm. I was sweating, a talking worm? I could barely breathe, it was so shocking.
"Well then wormy, what's your best offer?"

Tommaso Etemi (10)
Merton Court Preparatory School, Sidcup

The Forest

The light, fresh raindrops emulsify as they hit the uneven ground. Broad trees loom over the damp pathway, its leaves rustling as the wind brushes past them, like a painter creating an ethereal portrait of a wonderland for the living. The moon peeks her head from the east, its supple smile cools its surroundings. Everything goes silent, not wanting to break the picturesque view of the rays of the moon. *Her* soldiers surround her as she zooms across the sky. *Her* presence is, however, not noticed. As humanity is deep in its slumber, the owl's hooting in the night.

Joachim Wong (10)
Merton Court Preparatory School, Sidcup

The Teeth

White coarse sand followed me wherever I went. Tiny waves crashed onto the rocky cliffs. Seagull calls rang in my ears. "Caw! Caw!" The fragrance of salt wafted into my nose. The dampness in the air tickled my tongue... Then closer and closer something came and suddenly my mind went black. It looked like vampire's teeth. No matter how fast I fled, the teeth pursued me mercilessly. I gazed at the sky for a split second and it was darker than charcoal. The teeth surrounded me and closed in. "Deet!"
I bolted upright, it was a dream, or was it?

Onali Jayawardhena (10)
Merton Court Preparatory School, Sidcup

What A Magical Sight!

Once upon a time, there lived a girl called Helen. One morning she woke up and decided to go for a walk in the woods. When she entered the woods, she saw rainbow butterflies and neon-coloured dragonflies. As she walked deeper into the deep green, she found an array of flowers, violet daisies, scarlet roses, saffron dandelions and sparkly red, ruby poppies. It was mesmerising. Helen stepped further into the woods, passing luscious, velvet moss. Her steps were quick but very steady. Her heart beat loudly, echoing in her head. What she was about to see was just magical!

Priyanka Lall (10)
Merton Court Preparatory School, Sidcup

A Wander In The Woods

My family was on a long-awaited camping trip in an ancient forest. Whilst we were enjoying songs and marshmallows around the campfire, strange noises came from the forest. No one else heard them, just me, which was even stranger. It wasn't too dark yet so I slowly and calmly walked away from camp towards the noises. It was a slow creak followed by a sudden soft bang, again and again. Suddenly, I saw a large oak tree with a moving golden gate in its hollow. Forest fairies, the size of children, were flying gracefully through to a different long-awaited adventure.

Olivya Isaac (10)
Merton Court Preparatory School, Sidcup

The Glowing Woods

As I entered the woods, all the creatures went into hiding. The sky, trees and flowers began to fade. It was coming up to the darkest hour of the night. Everything suddenly became quiet. The crows came fluttering from the conifers. I looked up at the dreary sky, charcoal-black in colour. A distant clock suddenly struck twelve. It sounded like a bombshell. I sprinted forward aimlessly until I saw something, there was a bright light ahead of me. The moonlight was beaming on an open clearing. The whole area was glowing. I had to admit, it was beautiful scenery.

Aariya Patel (9)
Merton Court Preparatory School, Sidcup

The Strange Encounter

As I strolled through the woods with my dog, Coco, we were showered with leaves from above. Something was watching us but what and where from? I shuffled closer to Coco and carried on walking. Suddenly, there was a huge crash and a creature appeared! "Hello, dear," it said.

"Who are you and what do you want?" I asked.

"I am the one and only Zeena and I am here to steal your heart!" And with that, she grabbed me and Coco and we were suddenly in a dark, damp cave. Coco ran out barking and left me alone...

Elinor Micklefield (10)
Merton Court Preparatory School, Sidcup

Pooh Sticks

It had rained heavily the night before, the stream was flowing faster than ever. The ground was so soggy beneath us and the mud was squelchy. We had decided to play pooh sticks. We had all found the perfect sticks, thin, light and easy to throw. We shrieked as we threw them simultaneously. They disappeared underneath the bridge, out of sight. We raced to the other side, suddenly the loudest splash, Barney had jumped into the stream and protruded with one of his sticks. From this day on, we still don't know who won it.

Lilia White (10)
Merton Court Preparatory School, Sidcup

There Must Be A Way Out

Here I am, in a deep forest, alone in a gloomy, terrifying part of nowhere. The trees were staring at me like silent sentries. The trees in the forest were bladder-brown. The musty air was difficult to breathe. I needed to escape! Suddenly, I heard a rustle in the bushes. I began to slowly walk towards it. I found it was a wild horse! I began to stroke his back, it felt soft to the touch. I began to mutter under my breath, "Will you take me home?" He galloped through the vast and undisturbed forest to my home!

Sofia Sarvestani (10)
Merton Court Preparatory School, Sidcup

A Mystical Dream

I was in a forest, this one was magical. Not like a fairy tale, this felt real. It made me feel alive! Anyways, back on track, I was in a forest, there were deer prancing about, bunnies jumping merrily around me, chubby fish in a pond, and much more! It was like paradise. Even the birds were flying around me happily. I took a step forwards, the grass was jumping up and down, no word in the dictionary could describe how I felt, it was amazing. I took another step and then a million butterflies calmly landed on my nose.

Zara Enver (10)
Merton Court Preparatory School, Sidcup

Jack And The Mysterious Tree

It was getting dark, all the children were getting put to bed. Except for one child named Jack. Jack got out of bed and snuck out of his house. He went for a walk in the local woods. He had always been told not to go into the woods. He went in anyway. He could see lots of magical things like mushrooms made of marshmallows, chocolate rivers and a very special tree that could talk. The tree was telling him to stay forever, it then pulled him into the tree trunk. Was there any escape now? For Jack... hopefully!

Charlie Wilson (10)
Merton Court Preparatory School, Sidcup

The Pixie Forest

Dawn rose above the forest, highlighting the azure colour of the sky. The mist stayed on the ground like a cloaked cloud. I wandered into the emerald-green forest, listening to the chirpy dawn chorus, watching my feet as they skated on the carpet of leaves. Suddenly, out of the corner of my eye, I saw something running as quick as lightning. It startled me so much that I froze on the spot. It ran up the oak tree and looked upon me with wide eyes and a goofy smile. Wow, a Devon Pixie, this was amazing.

Freddie Kite (10)
Merton Court Preparatory School, Sidcup

Midnight At The Campsite

It was getting dark, I was worried about not getting back to the campsite by sunrise. This is why I should not go wandering in the woods on my own. It was getting dark and gloomy, I could hear owls calling out to each other. They sounded angry. Then I heard a cackle. I said to myself, "I recognise a sound like that, it's a bit like my evil stepmother's laugh." I had to get back quickly, as it sounded like she was up to no good. I was afraid for my dad. I was determined to get back.

Daisy Cormack (10)
Merton Court Preparatory School, Sidcup

A Wander In The Woods

I was wandering through the woods and I could hear infinite sounds. As I was trudging through the moist wilderness, I came across a bird next and got a snap of the eggs, little did I know an eager mother had come back from hunting and she was not happy. As I marched on, I caught a glimpse of a rare Hawaiian crow, I took a few pictures and went. After a while, I stopped to admire the blooming of the sun. Flowers, a truly magnificent sight. As I neared the end of my trek I saw a beehive then left.

Christiaan Datema (10)
Merton Court Preparatory School, Sidcup

Walking In The Forest

I was walking in the forest when I heard a noise. I looked behind me. Nothing was there. Suddenly, someone pulled my hair and turned me towards them. A bedraggled man with long shaggy hair was looking at me. He gagged me and tied me to a tree! I was terrified! He then blindfolded me and bound my hands. Was I going to die? I suddenly heard a sound. It was the sound of a knife being sharpened. Just then, I felt an agonising pain in my chest. What had happened? I began to feel dizzy, was I dead?

Satara Dhesi (10)
Merton Court Preparatory School, Sidcup

Siren Head Vs Wolf

Five days ago, there was a thing in the forest, this guy identified it as Siren Head. The government computers were saying that a giant wolf was heading there. There was a massive sound, it was the wolf trying to kill the Siren Head. It was interesting to watch. The wolf came in to attack. The signal got lost. We went to look. The Siren Head won but he was badly hurt. We took him back to our house. We helped him heal and took him back to the forest and he went back home to his family.

Ethan Pearce (10)
Merton Court Preparatory School, Sidcup

A Wander In The Woods

Winny woke up one foggy morning and decided to go for a walk in the woods. After she got dressed, Winny went to get her blue trainers on. Winny went into the dark woods, inside were tall green trees looking upon her. She was strolling through the leaves until she saw a long river. She went closer and there were some tadpoles peacefully swimming. After searching, she saw a fox eating its prey. Winny decided to go back home because it was late. Winny walked back home and went to bed.

Keeya Pindoria (10)
Merton Court Preparatory School, Sidcup

The Lunar Ninetail

It was getting dark, the husky's silver fur shimmered in the moonlight. It was the full moon. It was Midnighttail. The husky's bright purple eyes darted across the forest, looking into the darkness. "Shh, Starlight," whispered the crystal-haired girl, next to the husky. They heard a scream. "Quick. It's a ninetail! They ran to the howl. "It can't be... It's not possible." The girl's eyes widened. "This species should be extinct." Resting beneath her was a legendary lunar ninetail. she ran her hands against its fur, "It's wounded, but it's not fading." The legendary creature started purring.

Maryam Akhmedova (11)
Miles Coverdale Primary School, Shepherd's Bush

The Scary Figure

Once upon a time, there was a nine-year-old boy called Jeff. One day, Jeff was walking around in the woods for hours until he heard a very scary noise coming from behind him. Jeff slowly turned around and saw a very scary black figure. The black figure had red, scary eyes and tall pointy horns. "Argh!" screamed Jeff. Jeff tried to run but the tall figure teleported right in front of him. "What do you want from me?" asked Jeff.
"I want to kill you and rip your soul out and shred your bones into tiny little pieces."
"Why me?"

Ali Ahmad (11)
Miles Coverdale Primary School, Shepherd's Bush

Lost In The Woods

It was getting dark and the trees were getting closer and closer with each step we made. The noises we heard we couldn't see, they kept following us for a while. The rain came pouring on us with extreme lightning and banging sounds of thunder. How would we ever get out of these miserable woods and what would I use to get us out of here?
"Brother, where are we going?" said my sister nervously.
"We are going home."
And that is when a peek of light showed up but it wasn't freedom we wished before.

Retaj Ismail (11)
Miles Coverdale Primary School, Shepherd's Bush

The Hunted

It was getting dark as Houston and I approached the altar of the Sunne. We knew we didn't have time as the horde of monsters could be marching up the stairs. I gripped the pendant, a gift from my mother when she died a year ago. It was glowing a bluish colour. I'd always thought the pendant was a bearer of good tidings and luck. Houston panted as we reached the altar. It looked like a Chinese temple, with its silver chimes hanging on the pillars. A carved slab of stone lay in front. I placed the pendant in, *bang!*

Rayan Anwar (11)
Miles Coverdale Primary School, Shepherd's Bush

Be Careful What You Say

It was getting dark, my friend had left me in the woods by myself. There was that one creepy old lady staring at me. She asked me, "Are you lost, darling?"
"Of course I'm not lost, I'm strolling in the woods at night," I said sarcastically. I was lost and couldn't find my way out. The old lady asked where my parents were, they were at home. The lady offered to take me home and asked my address. As we were going home, I got kidnapped by the lady, that's why you don't say your address.

Musub Mohamoud (11)
Miles Coverdale Primary School, Shepherd's Bush

A Wander In The Woods

There must be a way out. There has to be. I'd read books about woods and the books said that every forest had a beginning and an ending. I was lost. Nowhere to go. I sat down by a lollipop tree. I started singing while adorable forest animals gathered around me to hear my voice. A lovely blackbird came flying and comfortably settled itself, sitting on my arm. When I stopped singing, I started talking about my life, my stepmother, how I miss my real parents. They started running towards a house. I was safe. I was at home.

Violett Guba (11)
Miles Coverdale Primary School, Shepherd's Bush

The Man With No Hands

I'd escaped but I was still not in the clear. It was meant to be an ordinary camping trip, but all of a sudden, it all went wrong. In the area that we picked to go camping, there were rumours of a camper that had been devoured by the Anger. For those of you that are not familiar with the tale of the Anger, it is a small species that clings onto humans, devouring them inside out and on rare occasions the Anger can control the lifeless husk and unfortunately I was currently looking at a man with no hands.

Zakaria Gherbi (11)
Miles Coverdale Primary School, Shepherd's Bush

The Sound

"There must be a way out," I said. Frantically searching, I was in the middle of the woods. I didn't know how I got there and how I should get out. I tried to remember but I could not. There was a lot of trees scattered together so I could barely see anything. I did not have my phone although I realised I was wearing a backpack on my back, which was quite strange because it was unfamiliar to me. I searched through it, but as I did, I heard something. My heart leapt. I stopped. What was that?

Farah Elfayoumy (11)
Miles Coverdale Primary School, Shepherd's Bush

The Ascension Of The Demon

It was getting dark, my family was scared because they knew every night a demon would come to eat one of us. It had already taken my sister, so this time we were prepared to kill it so we could avenge my sister's death. The door opened, we knew it was time, but suddenly, the door closed. We were all scared, even the demon, but then Dad crept up behind the demon and chopped its head off, we were relieved. Then my mom told me we were moving back to Chicago. I wished my sister was, rest in peace sister.

Nadir Zumrawy (11)
Miles Coverdale Primary School, Shepherd's Bush

The Man In The Woods

It was getting dark, I still couldn't find home. The time was ten o'clock, I was starving and thirsty, I'd been running for hours to get cherries and now I was stuck in one of the worst situations of my life. I found an abandoned cabin, as I was searching for supplies. I found a flare gun with one flare. I shot it in the air. No response. I was about to starve. Just as I was about to faint, I heard a noise, it sounded like a motor and it was heading for me, it was a helicopter.

Mustafa Abbasi (11)
Miles Coverdale Primary School, Shepherd's Bush

Escaping The Woods

There must be a way out of this! I rummaged through my bag for tools to help me escape from the woods. Here is how it all started. I was on a camping trip. It was approaching night-time and we were getting ready for bed. Then all of a sudden, a green figure grabbed me and took me into a place far away from the campsite. I was trying to escape. Out of nowhere, a black cat came with a cart. It took me away back to the campsite. I did not have the slightest idea of what happened.

Fatima Ali (11)
Miles Coverdale Primary School, Shepherd's Bush

A Moving Light In The Sky

In the distance, I saw a glowing dot while I was walking home, for the first few seconds I was confused about what it was. Then, I had an idea. I started running towards it to see what it was but it was still too far. I tried to guess what it was but the only thing that came up in my head was a star. I knew for a fact that it wasn't a star though, because it was moving towards me. so I waited for it to come closer to me, it was a turquoise, flying car.

Medina Makhloufi (11)
Miles Coverdale Primary School, Shepherd's Bush

Tigger's Amazing Adventure

"I'd finally arrived at the secret meeting place and knocked on the door five times, but they wouldn't let me in," said Tigger to Christopher. "Why didn't they let me in?" questioned Tigger.

"I don't know, but we will find out why," said Christopher.

He stormed off down to the large green oak tree and hit the door so hard it almost broke. Someone answered and *boom!* It was so loud it scared Tigger. They wandered in and everyone shouted, "Surprise!" It was a surprise party all this time. They partied all night.

Daisy-lou Czuczman (10)
Minster CE Primary School, Minster

A Wander In The Woods

In the distance, there is a humungous forest, as thick as the Amazon, crying for me to come in. As I stand there, the grass starts pushing me into the dark place of sorrow! Towering trees circle as I walk past. Flying squirrels that are really swift for their size, glide through the trees. I walk and walk but nothing yet, with gracious green all around, it's feeling quite boring now. As leaves start to fall and I see the dusk of dawk. I figure out I have been here for a year, with the winter breeze in the air.

Ameli Shaw (10)
Minster CE Primary School, Minster

A Wander In The Woods

It was getting dark when I saw it, a ghostly figure in the shadows. It had slimy, brown skin and long hind legs, large warts on its back and two beady, black eyes that seemed to bore right through you. I was in the woods when I saw it. I was wandering about, playing in the golden leaves when it appeared out of nowhere! It gave a horrible croak like a frog but it wasn't one. I ran back home as quick as lightning. My ma came with me and there it was again. Ma smiled. "That's a toad, silly!"

Toby Woodward (9)
Minster CE Primary School, Minster

The Kidnap

A stress-free wander in the woods quickly became a stressful chase. It all started when I heard a twig snap behind me. My heart stopped and my hands began to shake. I turned around and saw nothing. I started to walk again, wondering what might have made the noise, out of the blue, I heard the rustling of leaves, a foot hit the ground. I turned my head, as soft as a hawk in flight. A dark, intimidating figure stood before me. All of a sudden, I plunged into darkness, I'd been kidnapped!

Ella Hooper (11)
Minster CE Primary School, Minster

Impending Doom

It was getting dark, the worms of the forest woke, to illuminate the forlorn darkness. That's when I saw the boy, his emotionless face following the path below him, the silent crickets leaping from his relatively large strides. I knew it before it happened, as if the trees had whispered to me. An ear-splitting drone cracked the silence, the boy, now with a sense of panic, tired around, listening to the wolves baying for blood. He ran. I followed him on my laced wings. Travelling forward, we were confronted with a wall of roaring fire and vampire-wolves...

Samuel Garfoot (11)
Shirley Community Primary School, Cambridge

Smoke Cloud

One day, I woke up from a nightmare in the forest and there was this black smoke cloud with the widest array of jagged blood-red teeth and dark voids under his eyes like he had a bad night's sleep. I froze like I was paralysed. I couldn't move, the cloud started to move towards me. I ran, this had to be another dream, I couldn't be getting chased. I screamed. I was speeding up and its smile was getting wider. I was suffocating. I fainted and I woke up, but in another dimension. I was consumed.

Hapi Bonetti-Phillips (11)
Shirley Community Primary School, Cambridge

Christmas Is Here

It was getting dark, that Christmas Eve, so I went to bed. I was so excited for tomorrow.
In the morning I woke up to my mum and dad handing me a neatly wrapped present. On the label, it said 'Meg'. Oh sorry, I forgot to tell you I'm Meg by the way, a six-year-old girl. I opened my gift, I cried tears of joy, my own toy pony! Then I heard something, "Hello." I looked down, then up, my parents smiled. All of a sudden, I had a real-life talking horse standing next to me...

Poppy Janes (8)
St Francis Catholic Primary School, Maldon

Rising Legends

Rustle! I heard strange noises coming from the bushes around me, I had wandered too far from camp. Unsure of what to do, I just bolted, ouch. I'd tripped over something. All the trees were covered with blood, it wasn't even dry, but then from a pile of ashes rose, morphing glowing eyes that glared menacingly at me. Sprinting as fast as my legs could carry me, I spotted the edge of the forest in front of me. It was dawn. Narrowly escaping, the thing sizzled in the sunlight. I was safe, for now, wasn't I?

Harry Malone (10)
St George's CE Primary School, Wrotham

Mythical Beast

It was getting dark in the redwood forest, then Sam came to a cliffside. There was nowhere to run. "Huh, what's that?" Sam mumbled. Then he felt a cold breath down his neck. Before he could turn around he bolted, slipped and shrieked with pain because rocks dug into his back. Finally, the chase finished and the creature was nowhere to be seen! Up ahead he saw a hidden pick-up truck and limped over to it. Five seconds later, the brute attacked him. He ran and ran until he found a safe house. He ran inside...

Charlie Newbold (9)
St George's CE Primary School, Wrotham

Curious Cemetery

In the beginning, I saw in the distance a foggy cemetery. I was tempted to go in but it might be risky. Soon after a few minutes, I went inside and looked at a grave. It read 'James Abbott'. My name. I screamed. In a blink of an eye, wild animals were chasing me. I scurried away, eventually, I saw a train. I jumped onto it. I was happy to see my family again, also being back in my warm, cosy home. When I got out of my misery. I told my lovely family about my amazing adventure.

James Abbott (9)
St George's CE Primary School, Wrotham

The Woods

It was getting dark, me and my friends heard ghosts and forest spirits in a big, old abandoned church. Me, AJ and Benji sat outside of the church. It was fine until Benji went missing. Me and AJ went to search for Benji. We heard a ghost in the air. It said, "I will set you challenges to find your friend," so we accepted and found him. We found monsters. Benji chopped off his head, AJ stabbed one in the heart and I kung-fu kicked one in the head and hit it with a crowbar.

Blake Saunders (10)
St George's CE Primary School, Wrotham

The Horrific Adventure

As I lay in my bed, I heard a noise behind me. I sat up and turned around. I saw forest spirits floating in the air, mumbling shrieks of laughter. Suddenly, the floor started peeling away and then darkness. I had to do something quickly. With my dog, Hope, by my side, we ran into the forest. Not knowing where we were going, we ran in the opposite direction to the house. I was so nervous and Hope was whimpering. We came up to a cave, this was the last stopping point for us.

Benjamin Forsyth (10)
St George's CE Primary School, Wrotham

The Dark Woods

In the distance, I saw an abandoned church. As I got closer, there were gates around it. The gates were as black as leather boots. I heard something behind me. As I turned it was just Blake and Georgie and James R. When we saw how tall the gate was, we started to climb over. when we got down, someone or something in black tackled James R. We crept in. James was over a fire, we put out the fire. James got down and we never went back and went home.

Ryan Puttock (10)
St George's CE Primary School, Wrotham

The Axolotl World

There it was, the portal to the axolotl world. I walked in and I was amazed, there was so much coral which made light. I soon realised I was underwater. I swam up to the top of the cave as quick as I could but it soon collapsed on me but then ten thousand axolotls swam me to the top of the cave to their leader. The king axolotl knew how to speak English and asked me what I was doing there. I said I was there to learn about the fish.

James Richards (10)
St George's CE Primary School, Wrotham

It Was Dark

As I went through the tough gate, it started to get dark. The gate closed behind me. It was creepy. I heard a ghost spirit so I turned around and I couldn't see anything. I saw a ladder to climb the wall. I entered a graveyard. There was a massive hole in the floor. The other gate was open so I ran through the gate. I ran to my house and told my mum what I saw and heard.

Lucy Hodges (9)
St George's CE Primary School, Wrotham

Minotaur Town

It's too late, I thought, *it's coming.* It all started when I came into the town of the Minotaur, the Minotaur was half-man, half-bull. Anyways, I was on a quest and it just so happened I was crossing through a town of smaller, but stronger Minotaur. I'm a human so they threw me into the maze of the Minotaur and here I am after cheating death a few times. I was at the huge doors, banging on them. Eventually, the tower guards opened the doors, and I quickly ran so far. I did not return to the town.

Jamie Rooney McGuigan (10)
St Patrick's Primary School, Hilltown

Surviving The Woods

I've escaped, it's too late to turn back, I'm focusing on where to go next. I can feel my heart pumping hard in my chest, the sound of silence follows me. I keep on running, there's a gate, without thinking, I run in. Wow! This place is so amazing, so many big, bushy trees and big ponds with a bench and the birds tweeting and sticky sap running down the trees. I think to myself, *no one will find me here*, I might just try and survive in these woods. And that's just what I do.

Cara Cole (10)
St Patrick's Primary School, Hilltown

The Killer In The Woods

It was dark and I was getting lost. I was walking through the woods when I saw a small figure standing in the distance. I started to approach the figure and it was the prisoner that escaped three years back. He killed tonnes of people before and I thought I would die. I suddenly fell down a trap on a lot of dead bodies. I started to move them about and then one was alive. She started breathing rapidly and I got really scared. We were helping each other and we found a door, we opened it and escaped!

Erin Rooney (10)
St Patrick's Primary School, Hilltown

The Mystery People

It was getting dark and I was getting tired. I couldn't bear any longer without sleep. I had tried my best to stay awake but it was no use, so I looked around for some place to sleep and eventually, I found a cave.
When I woke up, I thought, *there has to be a way out!* I got up and looked around. I gathered my stuff up and left. Twenty-eight minutes later, I saw some people. They were looking for something or someone; were they looking for me? I ran and hid...

Jessie Maginn (10)
St Patrick's Primary School, Hilltown

Craziness In The Woods!

I'd escaped from the woods, not magical ones anyway. I got taken away by some tiny creatures. I didn't see them and they put me in a sack in a corner but they were not good at tying. I'd just realised that I was in a tree, when they weren't looking I got out. One of the creatures shouted at me. I was running, I saw the exit but it was shrinking, they threw a tiny spear and it hit my bum and I was so close and then shrank but I escaped from the creatures.

CJ Grant (10)
St Patrick's Primary School, Hilltown

The Forest Dream

The beautiful forest. I play in it every day. It has paths with wildflowers. There's a pond with a bridge. I go there every week. I went one day with my mum. She thought I was going mad. She saw nothing. I am attached to this forest. I get stuck. I am a part of the forest, nobody can help me. How can I get out? Why can I not get out? I find a cave... Suddenly I am in my bed, that was the most amazing and scary dream ever!

Beibhinn McPolin (10)
St Patrick's Primary School, Hilltown

Bull Attack!

I heard a bull behind me, I was scared. He came behind me and hit me with his head and kicked me. He jammed me up against a gate. I just got out, then jumped over the gate too. He hit me and kicked me, he hurt my neck and back and legs. I rang my friends Charlie and Roose to help me, they came and the bull saw them, the bull had a ring in its nose, we grabbed the ring and all of us took him down.

Tj McKay (10)
St Patrick's Primary School, Hilltown

The Mystery Woods

Once upon a time, there were three kids and they ran away from home. They didn't know where they were, they just wanted to stay away from their mum. They arrived at a mysterious place. There was a lot of howling, they thought they saw a monster.

"Sarah, are you sure about this?"

"Yes," said Sarah.

They went deeper in and they saw animals running past them. They were intimidated. After an hour they saw a witch.

"Hello," said the witch. The witch made a potion. "Drink it, kids."

Their mum came and said, "No!"

They apologised to her.

Mathushi Manoharan (9)
St Thomas A Becket Catholic Primary School, Eastbourne

Dream Or Not?

It was getting dark. Kyle, Kylar and Stacy saw a mysterious fog. They approached the fog without holding back. But little did they know, there was a sign that said, 'Do Not Enter'. The fog was thick and it was hard to see.
"Kyle, brother, are you sure this was a good idea?" whispered Kylar. Although he didn't listen, Stacy just shrugged. A gush of wind swooped across them. But then they heard a noise. They stepped back twice. All of them screamed and ran as far as they could, then realised it was just a dream or was it?

Eunice Macaranas (10)
St Thomas A Becket Catholic Primary School, Eastbourne

The Forest

One day, three kids were wandering in the woods. Twins called Corlien, Kyle and their friend Stacy. They loved playing in the woods. Then Corlien saw an unknown creature, then Stacy saw it. The creature had deer antlers, green hair with flowers in it. Then Kyle saw the beast and slashed it with his long, sharp stick. Corlien pushed Kyle over on the dirty ground and ran into the deep, dark forest. Then Stacy yelled out for Corlien and ran for her. Kyle got up from the ground and ran after them.

Henry Leek (9)
St Thomas A Becket Catholic Primary School, Eastbourne

Island Disco

Once upon a time, there was a little sailer called Tim. He had a blue boat that he sailed every day. He lived on an island all by himself. He felt bored and sad. He decided to have a disco. He sailed to his friends' houses to invite them. First, he went to Dilly the duck and she said yes. Then he went to Sam the fish and he said yes. Then he went to Jake the seahorse and he said yes. The four friends had the best time ever. They went to the movies and had popcorn.

George Prince (9)
St Thomas A Becket Catholic Primary School, Eastbourne

Alien Attack

Clang! I had stepped on a shiny green button whilst I was having a walk in the woods. Suddenly, out of nowhere, a magical portal appeared. I accidentally tripped and fell into the portal. I was swirling and twirling until I ended up in outer space. I could breathe in zero gravity. It was astonishing! Out of nowhere, a green alien started to chase me! Another one too, until a pack of them appeared. I ran towards a spaceship. I flew around, trying to find the secret portal. Phew! That was close! I had escaped the aliens.

Sehjta Chauhan (8)
Talavera Junior School, Gun Hill

The Dark Woods

Once upon a time, there lived a boy named Jack. He planned to go into the woods. So that night, when he was leaving, he tripped over a stick, "Ouch," cried Jack.
"Are you okay?" someone asked.
"Yes thanks," said Jack.
"Okay," said the person.
Jack got up, he saw something in the distance, he couldn't hear anything, just twigs breaking and snapping and people moving bushes. Later, something jumped out of the bush, it was a ghost but Jack found out that the ghost was friendly, so Jack became friends with the ghost.

Amelia Southern (9)
Unity Academy, Blackpool

Fairy Devil Unicorn Named Athene

As I arrived at the secret meeting place, I saw, standing there, a zombie unicorn and the unicorn screamed, "Neigh, I'm a fairy unicorn and a devil unicorn too." If you got on the wrong side of her she would try to kill you but if you were good to her you would get a sweet. The sweet was a poisonous sweet. She didn't like giving away her sweets. So if she would she'd trap you for her dinner. Especially children. I found out her name. Athene. She ended up being my friend, but she was a kind zombie unicorn.

Mia Thornber (9)
Unity Academy, Blackpool

The Mind Control Powers

Once upon a time, there was a witch who had mind-control powers on everyone except James. He was playing hide-and-seek and had the best hiding spots so the witch couldn't cast a spell on him. Without being seen, James crept to the witch's hideout. James saw the machine. The witch was powering the machine. James used pliers to cut the wire, without a shock. Luckily the witch used all its power to power the machine so the witch was vulnerable. Just then, the army came and locked the witch in an underground dungeon.

Jack Fearon (8)
Unity Academy, Blackpool

The Secrets Of Atlantis

"There must be a way out of this bunker," shouted the head agent.
"The bunker is sinking," shouted the assistant. Finally, they reached a door, but it was the exit, then they saw the lost world of Atlantis. They had to report his back to their master but there was no service. All of a sudden, something touched the head agent's shoulder. He looked back and it was a serpent creature with scales and a fish tail, he took them to a fine underwater castle and then it took them to a great statue.

Kacey Coulter (9)
Unity Academy, Blackpool

Mia And The Unicorn

I heard a noise behind me, a horse noise. My mum shouted to me to come inside, I told my mum what I heard in the forest, I said, "It might have been a unicorn."
My mum said, "Go to bed, Mia,"
I said, "Okay."
My mum was watching TV. I snuck downstairs to go into the forest. I ran. I stopped because I saw a portal. I went in the portal and I saw lots of unicorns so I got one and called it Unicorn. Unicorn was rainbow with wings and a horn and we became best friends.

Athena Mann (9)
Unity Academy, Blackpool

The Man In The Jungle

It was getting dark and there was a man lost in the jungle. People kidnapped him and put him there. The man was screaming for help until he found an abandoned aeroplane. He checked the aeroplane all around. He tried to fix it but it was no use. At midnight, he slept on the plane so nothing could hurt him. In the morning, he went on a journey. About two hours later, he found an old jungle temple. On the way out, he found fireworks which he set off and people saw it on a ship, so they saved him.

Jack William Jones (10)
Unity Academy, Blackpool

The Dead Man

One day, I was on the beach and I tripped on a rock. I decided to dig it up but it was a dead man. I called the police and they said, "We'll be five minutes," so I went to skim rocks but when I came back he was gone so I got six years in prison. After my six years in prison, when I got home, I looked out the window and I saw the man. I went back to the beach and the man was there but I didn't see the sword which chopped my head off.

Lewis Geoghegan (9)
Unity Academy, Blackpool

Captured

I saw a portal. I walked along the path and eventually made it to the portal. I stepped into the portal and a goblin caught me. I woke up in jail and saw a key so I tried to grab it. Luckily, my arm was long enough. I opened the jail and ran back to the woods and through the portal. When I got home, I told my parents what happened. They told me never to go back. I never did, never again.

Kila Murphy (9)
Unity Academy, Blackpool

The Angry Bear And The Man

I found a secret base and walked up and saw an angry bear with a bag. The bear pressed a button and went underground. I followed the angry bear then I saw one hundred more angry bears so I ran out but I got caught and was thrown in a cage and locked up. I could not move and I was scared so I wiggled and I got out. I found a key and got out but the angry bear was sleeping so I escaped.

Harry Abraham (10)
Unity Academy, Blackpool

A Wander In The Woods

I heard a noise. Twigs snapping wherever I turned, shaking me, with absolute fear, draining my happiness. Running away, I hid behind a big rock and hoped it would just pass. There was heavy breathing getting louder and louder. I was trying to find my friends to warn them. The sound got heavier and heavier. I guessed it was a monster. No matter how hard I tried, the monster got quicker. My heart almost skipped a beat. It hugged me! Looking behind, it was my friends, we all laughed harder and harder about the mighty, strong monster!

Mena Chaiyapantho (8)
Windhill Primary School, Mexborough

A Wander In The Woods

I heard a noise whilst lost in the woods. Heavy breathing, something or someone was watching me from the underground. I froze like a rabbit waiting for a fox to pounce. I was rummaging through the leaves. My hands were shaking as I got closer and closer to the source, not knowing what I would find. I went on my knees. The breathing stopped. I leaned forward and heard laughing. The creature emerged from the bushes and made me jump. It was my mum in disguise and my dog dressed as a werewolf. I was furious!

Ava Law (8)
Windhill Primary School, Mexborough

Night For A Knight

It was getting dark as I made it to the perfect clearing for a camp. Quickly, I set up my tent, sat down in front of it and made a campfire. Due to the gloom, my armour grew cold. I took it off and placed a few wooden poles over the fire. All was silent as I placed my silver armour over the rack. Suddenly, twigs started to snap. Was it my enemies? I grabbed my sword, opening the bushes. Relief filled my gut, as a white rabbit bounded out. My enemies shall feel my wrath tomorrow.

George Farthing (8)
Windhill Primary School, Mexborough

A Wander In The Woods

In the distance, I saw a really creepy church. Full of too much curiosity, I went in to explore it. Once I got in I realised it was abandoned in the eerie dark woods. With a big tug, I tried to open the door but it was locked. Then a pitch-black figure appeared, looking at me. It was a demon. I ran away while it was chasing me. Then I found a staff and when I held it, it was so bright, the demon vanished. After that, a ghost appeared and gave me a map of the dark woods.

Jashan Kaur (7)
Windhill Primary School, Mexborough

The Escape Room

There must be a way out, thought Jodi, as she peered around the room, there was only a carrier bag and suitcase. Jodi thought she should try to pick the lock like in the movies. But that failed so she got the carrier bag and twisted it around the handle. Just as Jodi was about to break the door down, *beep, beep!* Jodi awoke in a cold sweat. *It was just a dream*, she thought, as she looked at the time that said 10am. "I'm late for school!" Jodi shouted. She sprinted out of the house, what a weird dream.

Isabella Ashford (10)
Ysgol Gymraeg Caerffili, Caerphilly

The Trick In The Woods

Lily and Lewis went camping with their parents. Their friends warned them about a monster that lurked in the woods, but Lily and Lewis didn't believe them. Lily and Lewis had just finished unpacking, so decided to go for a walk. It was getting dark. They heard a noise behind them. "Argh!" screamed Lily. They both ran like cheetahs. Suddenly, they heard laughing. "Huh?" they both said. Lily and Lewis looked behind them and saw their school friends Harry and Isabella playing a trick on them. From that day forward, Lily and Lewis never went camping again.

Briallen Davies (9)
Ysgol Gynradd Gymunedol Gymraeg Llantrisant, Miskin

YOUNG WRITERS INFORMATION

We hope you have enjoyed reading this book – and that you will continue to in the coming years.

If you're a young writer who enjoys reading and creative writing, or the parent of an enthusiastic poet or story writer, visit our website **www.youngwriters.co.uk/subscribe** to join the World of Young Writers and receive news, competitions, writing challenges, tips, articles and giveaways! There is lots to keep budding writers motivated to write!

If you would like to order further copies of this book, or any of our other titles, then please give us a call or order via your online account.

Young Writers
Remus House
Coltsfoot Drive
Peterborough
PE2 9BF
(01733) 890066
info@youngwriters.co.uk

Join in the conversation!
Tips, news, giveaways and much more!

YoungWritersUK @YoungWritersCW @YoungWritersCW